The Totem Water Buffalo

ISBN: 1-4392-4001-9
ISBN-13: 978-1439240014

The Totem Water Buffalo

Written and Illustrated by Diana Clark

Also by Diana Clark
Sarah and the Golden Earring
Clearwater Girl

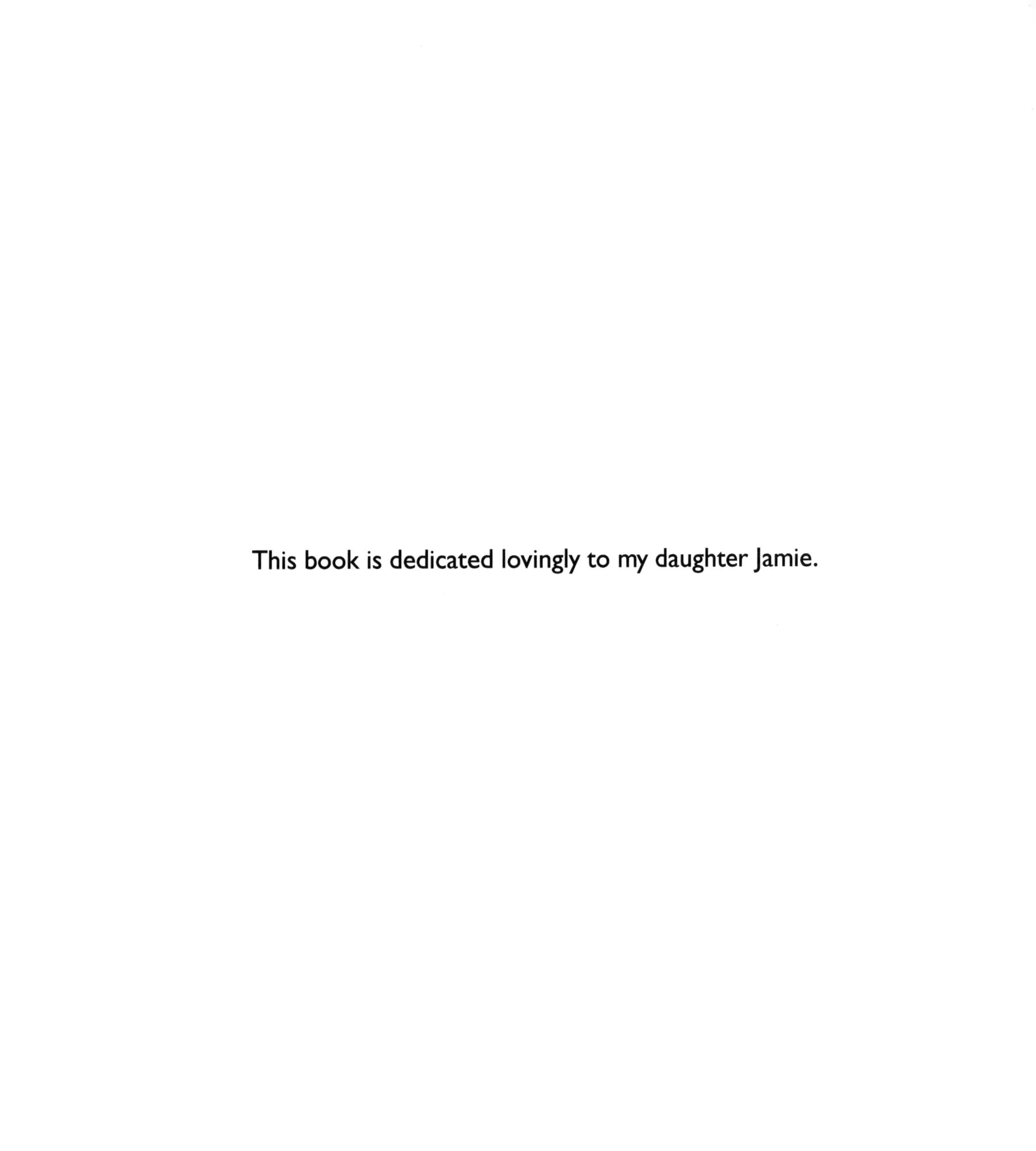

This book is dedicated lovingly to my daughter Jamie.

Acknowledgement:
I would like to thank my family and friends for their support and encouragement.
A special thank-you to Sigrid Gatens.

In a small village, surrounded by rice fields, lived a young boy named Chang. Chang was very free-spirited. He loved to have fun and to play with his friends. Everyone liked him very much.

Each day Chang had chores that he had to do before he could go play. He was responsible for the care of the small rice field next to his home.

All of this hard work was possible because he had the help of a water buffalo named Totem. Totem had belonged to his family since he could remember.

Totem was very strong and powerful. He was treated as the family pet because of his gentle nature.

After a hard days work, Chang would take Totem down to the pond for a swim as his reward for all his hard work.

Chang wore a necklace around his neck that was a hand-carved water buffalo. His Grandfather had given the necklace to him. The totem represented dependability, strength, and determination.

As Chang was growing older he became easily distracted because he could only think of playing with his friends.

One day after Chang was done working in the field, he saw his friend waving to him from the road. They had planned to go to town together to take part in the dragon parade.

Chang hurried and put Totem in his pen and ran inside the house to change his clothes. He left Totem all muddy.

With a sad face, Totem waited patiently to get his reward for his hard days work.

Chang did not take the time to let Totem have his daily swim. Totem was uncomfortable and paced back and forth in his pen.

When they arrived in town the boys had a great time. They joined in with the annual Parade of Dragons.

The dragons were very colorful. The boys had so much fun! Afterwards, they headed home.

Chang waved goodbye to his friend and walked past Totems' pen. From the corner of his eye he could not see Totem and he realized that in his haste he had left the gate open.

Chang called out for Totem but there was no sign of the water buffalo. He was now very worried.

Many thoughts were in his head; what would he tell his parents? How would he get his work done? How could they ever replace Totem?

Chang was so frustrated. He yanked the necklace from his neck and threw it across the lawn. His Mom was calling him to come in for dinner, "Chang, dinner is ready!"

Chang walked in the house, washed his hands, and changed his clothes. He sat down at the dinner table with his head hung low. He made no eye contact with his parents.

“What is wrong?” asked his Mom. Although it was difficult, Chang told the truth and explained what had happened. His parents had taught him to always be truthful and honest.

His parents were disappointed that Chang had not taken care of his responsibilities, but they were very proud that he told the truth. His Dad said they would help look for Totem after dinner. They all left to search for Totem.

After awhile Chang became so discouraged. He sat at the edge of a rice field on a big boulder. He was so sad and upset and his eyes filled with tears.

Off in the distance he heard a sound. Chang lifted his head and looked around.
In the old pond he saw Totem lying in the water.

Chang sprang to his feet and ran to Totem. He crawled on Totem's back and was so happy!

Chang gave Totem a big hug. He promised to always take care of Totem and they headed back home.

Chang thought back on all his wonderful memories with Totem. They were a great team together!

His parents had just returned home as Chang arrived. Chang saw his necklace in the grass and stopped to pick it up.

From that day forward, Chang was always responsible and reliable when it came to his chores and especially when it came to Totem's care. Chang was a boy you could depend on!

The End.

Made in the USA